ORCHARD BOOKS

First published in Great Britain in 2017 by The Watts Publishing Group

1 3 5 7 9 10 8 6 4 2

A CIP catalogue record for this book is available from the British Library

ISBN 978 1 40835 019 5

Printed and bound in China

Orchard Books
An imprint of Hachette Children's Group
Part of The Watts Publishing Group Limited
Carmelite House
50 Victoria Embankment
London EC4Y 0DZ
An Hachette UK Company

www.hachette.co.uk
www.hachettechildrens.co.uk

Licensed by:

The Secret of Gabby Gums

ORCHARD

The holidays were over and today the Cutie Mark Crusaders were back at school.

"I can't believe we didn't get our cutie marks during the summer," sighed Sweetie Belle.

"Featherweight got his!" moaned Scootaloo. "Why not us?"

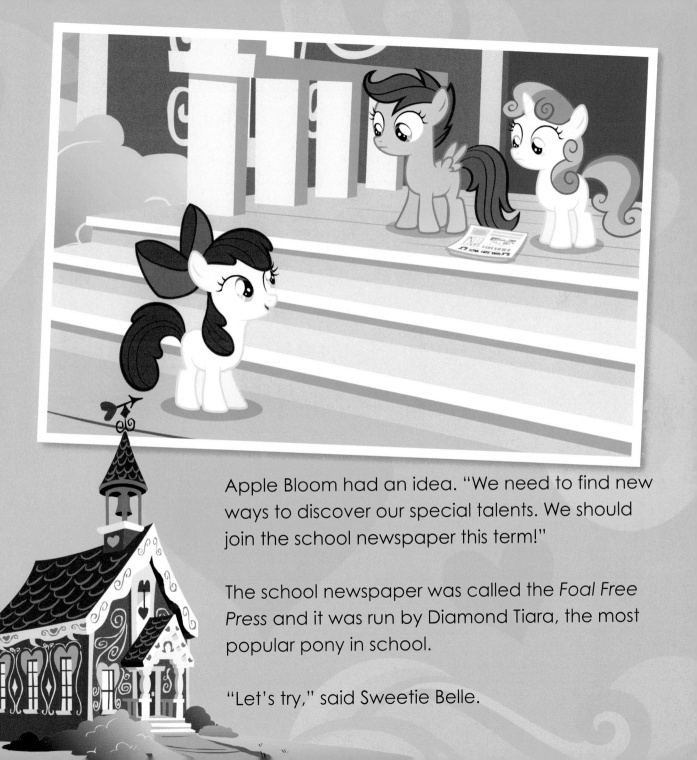

Apple Bloom had an idea. "We need to find new ways to discover our special talents. We should join the school newspaper this term!"

The school newspaper was called the *Foal Free Press* and it was run by Diamond Tiara, the most popular pony in school.

"Let's try," said Sweetie Belle.

Diamond Tiara was holding
a newspaper meeting that
very evening. The Cutie Mark
Crusaders listened nervously
as she explained her plans.

"Ponies, I want the juiciest
stories to fill these pages, and
the best gossip in Ponyville!
Can you do it?"

The Cutie Mark Crusaders set to work. They spent the week writing articles:

Apple Bloom interviewed Granny Smith about Ponyville in the olden days.

Scootaloo wrote a story about newborn animals.

Sweetie Belle asked Rarity to talk about her new hat design.

But Diamond Tiara wasn't happy.

"These reports are boring," she yelled. "I don't care about history or animals or hats. I want gossip – the juicier the better. I want new stories by the end of the day!"

"How are we going to find three great stories by the end of the day?" wailed Scootaloo.

Just then, Sweetie Belle spotted something. "Quickly, take a photo!" she told Featherweight.

The picture was very embarrassing! Snips and Snails were stuck together with a giant blob of bubble gum. "Diamond Tiara will love this!" giggled Sweetie Belle.

And she did! In fact she put it on the front page of the paper . . .

SNIPS AND SNAILS AND
BUBBLEGUM TAILS

Best of all, the Cutie Mark Crusaders had invented a name for themselves – Gabby Gums – so no one knew who had written the story!

The next day, everypony in school was talking about Snips and Snails. They pretended not to be embarrassed, but secretly they were very upset.

Diamond Tiara was delighted. "You are my top gossip columnists!" she told the Crusaders. "I want more stories like that one."

"Maybe this is our true talent!" cheered Scootaloo.

Sweetie Belle agreed. "If we write more Gabby Gums stories, I know we'll earn our cutie marks. Come on, ponies, let's get to work!"

Sweetie Belle, Scootaloo and Apple Bloom searched Ponyville for more gossip. No secrets were safe!

TROUBLE IN PARADISE? LOUD CRYING HEARD COMING FROM HOME OF POUND AND PUMPKIN CAKE...

TRICKS UP HER SLEEVE! WE REVEAL THE GREAT AND POWERFUL SECRETS OF TRIXIE!

Soon Gabby Gums wasn't just the talk of Ponyville School, she was a hit all over town! The ponies of Ponyville couldn't wait to get their hooves on the latest edition of the *Foal Free Press* with its juicy gossip and embarrassing stories!

At the beauty salon, Twilight Sparkle and her friends were talking about Gabby Gums. "These stories are teaching young ponies that it's funny to embarrass other ponies," sighed Twilight.

"But Gabby Gums is so funny!" laughed Applejack.

"Gabby Gums should have more respect for other ponies' privacy," argued Twilight. "It's not fair to share embarrassing secrets with the entire town."

And across town, three small ponies were starting to feel guilty . . .

"We want to stop writing nasty stories," Apple Bloom told Diamond Tiara. "We don't want to upset our friends."

"Absolutely not!" yelled Diamond Tiara. "Our readers love Gabby Gums' stories. I want more, more, more!"

Oh dear! The Cutie Mark Crusaders were sad. This didn't feel like a nice way to earn their cutie marks.

But things were about to go from bad to worse. The townsponies were starting to get angry about Gabby Gums' stories:

PINKIE PIE IS AN OUT-OF-CONTROL PARTY ANIMAL!

APPLEJACK: ASLEEP ON THE JOB!

FLUTTERSHY HAS TAIL EXTENSIONS!

TWILIGHT SPARKLE: I WAS A CANTERLOT SNOB!

"This gossip is upsetting everypony!" cried Twilight Sparkle, crossly.

When Rarity saw a story about her secret diary she was furious, and she realised that there was only one possible culprit . . .

Her sister Sweetie Belle had stolen her diary! Sweetie Belle and her friends must be Gabby Gums! Uh-oh!

Immediately, Rarity confronted her sister. "How could you do this to me, Sweetie Belle?" she fumed. "You're hurting people and spreading lies! Gabby Gums' nasty news is making ponies feel awful!"

It wasn't long before word spread that the Cutie Mark Crusaders were behind the Gabby Gums stories. Everypony began ignoring Sweetie Belle, Apple Bloom and Scootaloo.

The Cutie Mark Crusaders realised
something important: making people
feel bad was not the way to earn a
cutie mark!

It was time to apologise and win their
friends back . . . and Sweetie Belle had
a great idea about how to do it.

It was time for Gabby Gums to write one last article, telling the whole truth.

To tHe CitiZens of PonyVille:

I want to apologise for the embarrassment and upset I've caused. My column was actually written by Sweetie Belle, Apple Bloom and Scootaloo. We wanted to earn our cutie marks so badly that we forgot to be kind. But we promise from now on to respect the privacy of others and not to spread harmful gossip. We hope you'll forgive us, everypony.

Signing off for the last time,
Gabby Gums

Sweetie Belle, Apple Bloom and Scootaloo delivered a copy of the paper to all their friends and family, who forgave them with a hug.

They had learned a valuable lesson. Kindness and friendship were the way to earn their cutie marks – and they knew they would succeed eventually!